MW01141905

The Birthday Candle

by Jamie Bobo

Illustrations by Debbie Byrd

Allie Harper,
Happy 1st Birthday!
May this be the first of
many wonderful birthday
celebrations! :D:
Jamie Bobo

The Birthday Candle
Published by Yawn's Publishing
198 North Street
Canton, GA 30114
www.yawnspublishing.com

Library of Congress Control Number: 2014922715

ISBN: 978-1-940395-73-9 paperback,
        978-1-940395-74-6 eBook,
        978-1-940395-75-3 hardcover

Printed in the United States of America

The whimsical tale of how the
birthday candle
became a tradition.

Once upon a time, in the kingdom of Euwawa, there was an amazing young princess named Margolet. It was a very special day in Euwawa because it was Princess Margolet's birthday.

The royal family had planned a huge birthday celebration under the guidance of the most talented party planner, Princess Brooklyn, Margolet's older sister.

The entire kingdom had gathered at the palace for the grand celebration.

The guests were truly enjoying themselves with all the food, dancing, and socializing, but the highlight of the evening was the birthday cake!

And a grand cake it was! Princess Brooklyn had designed the masterpiece and had arranged for the best baker in all the land to create the most magnificent cake ever for her sister.

The party guests were so excited when the cake was rolled out; they went wild! The band started playing "Happy Birthday" as the king presented the cake to Princess Margolet. Just as the king was about to lead his kingdom in song, a terrible thing happened. The power went out.

It was completely dark.

The kingdom was silent while the king explained to the princess that the party would have to be over as they could not serve the cake in the dark.

Just then, the queen had an idea.

When she was coronated she was given a beautiful, single candle as a gift from the people of the neighboring kingdom. She could light that candle, so at least Princess Margolet could see the beautiful cake.

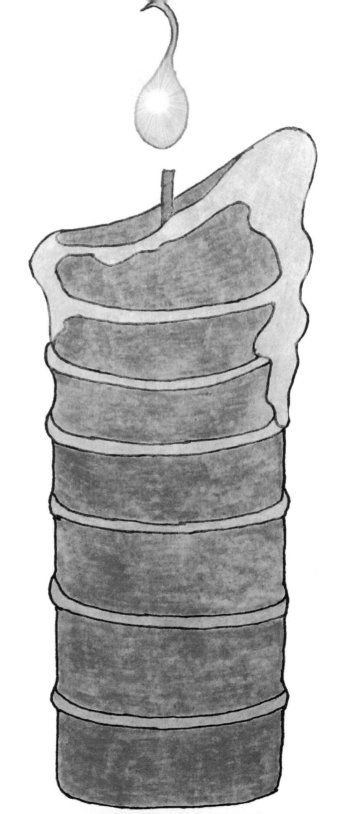

Quickly, the queen went to get the candle, lit it, and decided to place it right on top of the cake to illuminate it.

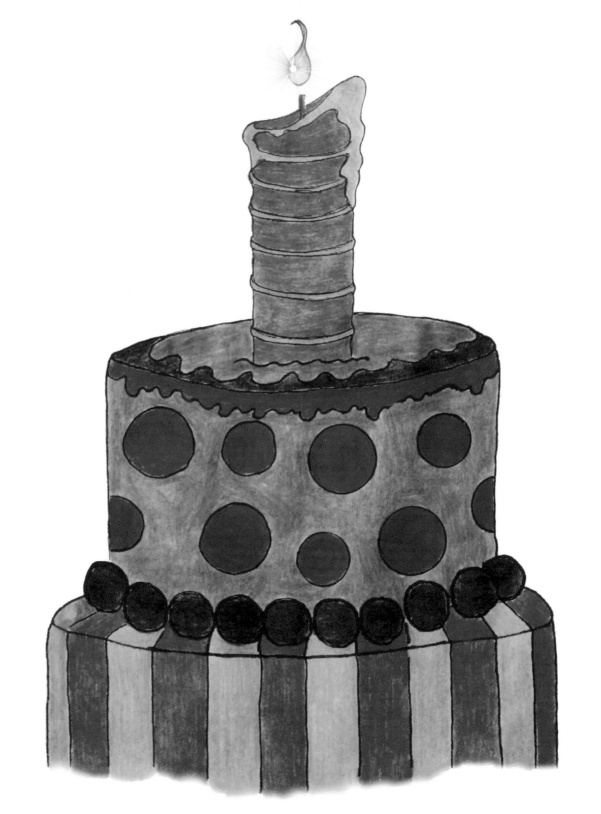

Then, the most amazing thing happened! Just as Princess Margolet stepped up to the cake to see its splendor, she made a silent wish that the power would come back on. And it did!!!

She then blew out the candle and the entire kingdom continued the celebration, complete with cake.

Jamie is a native of Canton, Georgia where she lives with her husband & two daughters.
A former elementary school teacher, she was encouraged by her family to put "The Birthday Candle" in writing.
She hopes you enjoy reading it as much as she enjoyed writing it!

Visit her at
www.thebirthdaycandle.com